Dedicated To

Parker & Evan

I have a BIG Problem!

I lost my last pair of underwear!

They're not under here.

They aren't under the window. Where did they go?

I GIVE UP!
I've looked everywhere!
I'll NEVER wear underwear again!

What are you yelling about?

I can't find my underwear anywhere.

Are you SURE you looked everywhere?

You have seen my underwear?
I HAVE seen your underwear.

Where did you see my underwear?
I saw your underwear under there.

Under where?
Yes. Your underwear.

Where is my underwear?
I saw your underwear under your bed.

I did not see my underwear when I put my head under my bed.

Did you look for your underwear under your dresser?

I looked under my dresser, but only saw a spider.

Did you look for your underwear under your window?

I did look for my underwear under my window
but my underwear is still a no show.

Where could my underwear be?
Don't ask me!

Hey! Look!
Under there! Under the chair!

It's MY underwear!
It's YOUR underwear!

"YES!!!"

What are you guys yelling about?

We found my underwear.
Underneath his chair.
Under where?

Oh, brother.